Worlds Afire

Worlds Afire

Paul B. Janeczko

CANDLEWICK PRESS
CAMBRIDGE, MASSACHUSETTS

Although the poems in this book are based on a historical incident, they are mainly works of fiction. While some describe people who were involved in the tragic events of that July afternoon, I have changed their names and imagined what they felt or said. Other characters are composites, based on several people. And some are strictly fiction.

First edition 2004

Library of Congress Cataloging-in-Publication Data

Janeczko, Paul B.
Worlds afire / Paul B. Janeczko. — 1st ed.
p. cm.
Summary: In this collection of eyewitness poems, the excitement and anticipation of attending the circus on July 6, 1944, in Hartford, Connecticut, turns to horror when a fire engulfs the circus tent, killing nearly 170 people, mostly women and children.
ISBN 0-7636-2235-4
1. Fires—Connecticut—Hartford—Juvenile fiction. [1. Fires—Connecticut—Hartford—Fiction. 2. Circus—Fiction.] I. Title.
PZ7.J2347 Wo 2004
[Fic]—dc21   2003055337

2   4   6   8   10   9   7   5   3

Printed in the United States of America

This book was typeset in Bulmer MT.

Candlewick Press
2067 Massachusetts Avenue
Cambridge, Massachusetts 02140

visit us at www.candlewick.com

To the memory of Thomas Barber,
Hartford Police Department detective,
who never forgot Little Miss 1565
and
in memoriam
Cindy Carroll
1950–2003

—Part 1—

Buddy Mullens

Twenty-Four-Hour Man

I arrive

the day before

when there is no circus,

only dreams of one

in the hearts of kids.

Without me

they would only wish

for the "Greatest Show on Earth."

They call me the "make sure guy."

I make sure the lot is laid out,

midway, menagerie,

big top, dressing tent;

make sure hay bales are stacked,

grain sacks piled,

gasoline and food delivered.

Make sure it's all there

before the train steams into town

tomorrow morning.

After I make sure

we'll be ready

for clowns

and wild beasts

and high-wire walkers,

I tramp the neighborhoods

and make sure the advance man

has plastered banners

where the kids can hear

the bright bold letters and a roaring tiger

calling them

to a show they'll never forget.

Willard Owens
Circus Buff

If I leaned out the bathroom window

I had the perfect view

across Barbour Street.

(But didn't the wife call me "fool"

when she saw me there.)

Haven't missed a circus in forty-two years,

like the wife never missing a white sale.

The Flying Squadron came first—

always—

carrying animal cages

cookhouse wagons

trucks

tractors

and noble elephants to move it all.

Razorbacks unloaded the flats

and the slow procession

wagons and elephants

trundled down Main to the lot.

First up is the cookhouse —

circus fellas can really pack it away —

with its long tables

red-checked tablecloths.

Horse tent next.

Hammer gangs pound

the stakes for the tents:

big top, sideshow, dressing room, shop.

The roughnecks come with the second section,

rolling out the big top

(and that's the perfect name for it —

newspaper called it the largest in the world,

all three blocks of it),

then lacing the canvas sections

together with rope.

When the tent is hoisted

to the top of the poles—

must be a good sixty feet—

canvasmen fasten the sidewalls,

like curtains on a stage,

'cept these lower from the top

to let in a breeze—

near 100 degrees in there—

and are spiked to the ground

to keep kids from sneaking in.

Can't say I blame 'em.

Tried it myself enough when I was a boy.

Never wanted to miss the show.

Dixie Levine

Gorilla Attendant

I can't remember

how I wound up with the circus,

let alone watching

Gargantua and Toto.

My job was to stand

in front of their air-conditioned wagon

(always 76 degrees, thank you)

under the sign that boasted

Largest Gorilla Ever Exhibited

and keep kids from banging on the glass.

Mostly, though, kids just stared at Gargy.

"Hey, mister," they'd say, "is he mean?"

I'd lean close to them and almost whisper,

"He hates humans."

They'd look at him

then back at me when I said,

"That's because his keeper beat him."

They'd take a small step back.

"Yep, can't say how many trainers he crippled.

Lost count."

"Really?"

I'd just nod sadly, afraid

I'd laugh at my own tales.

But nobody comes to the circus for the truth.

Am I right?

I mean, you tell me,

how many people want to know

Gargy swills Coca-Cola from a dented tin bowl?

That he couldn't care less about Toto,

if you catch my drift.

And that glass?

They put that in because people complained

when Gargy peed in his hand

and drenched the crowd.

Trust me.

Nobody comes to the circus for the truth.

Polly McDonald

Eleven Years Old

I'd've been happy to stay

in the animal tent all day,

but Aunt Betty insisted

we see the show

for the clowns and high-wire acts.

If you ask me,

walking the wire is nothing

compared to working the cage

with six jags and leopards

happy to slash your face

or take your arm.

So I made sure I saw

all the animals before the show.

Betty Lou, the pygmy hippo,

floated in her tank

while one of the cage boys —

exactly the job I want —

was feeding her

pieces of chocolate.

I swear.

Edith, the giraffe, made my neck hurt

from looking at her face so high.

I kept my distance

from the camels.

I've read they spit.

Even if you were blind and deaf,

you could know by the smell

you were with the animals.

By the time I saw the elephants

Aunt Betty was anxious

to get inside the big top.

Still, I had to stop

and admire them.

Lined up

they seemed to block the sun.

They're saggy animals:

the way their ears flap,

skin hangs,

trunks swing slowly from side to side,

then dart down to scoop a snack of hay.

I reached out

and offered a handful of peanuts.

In a blink they were snorted away.

I laughed

wiped my wet hand

on the seat of my pants.

I would've stayed

but Aunt Betty'd never forgive me

if we were late for the show.

Thomas Barber

Detective, Hartford Police Department

I was there to watch

for runaways

bail jumpers

smalltimers.

Anything that might ruin it

for the kids.

They could contain themselves

no longer,

the children whose fathers

were working overtime in a war plant

or fighting in foreign lands.

They broke free of mothers and aunts

in cotton dresses,

summer hats, purses in hand,

drawn to the rowdy serenade of the midway.

Wagons striped with red and white

sold orangeade

hot dogs

cotton candy the size of a hornet's nest

apples shelled by bright red candy

popcorn in boxes

peanuts in bags.

The ice-cream vendor's hand vanished

into the mist of his refrigerator truck,

then appeared

holding a bar or cone.

The bug men walked

beneath sandwich boards

selling chameleons

on string leashes

for half a buck.

Pennants

buttons

pictures of the sideshow, circus stars, the big top

miniature sombreros

and a monkey on a stick.

Money was tight

because of the war

but children gawked

grinned

and babbled to their friends,

captives of the riches

around them.

Harry King

United States Army

When the Red Cross volunteers

came for us,

they told us

the circus would take our minds off things.

Things

they couldn't speak of.

A best friend who died crying

like a baby in your arms,

a shy kid who lost half his head

to a sniper's bullet,

the bigmouth who bragged

until we hit the beach

and he died, legless, in disbelief.

So we went to the circus

but it didn't take our minds off things

not as we moved among the stares,

reminders of letters unanswered,

men buried far from home.

But, except for Ed

in a wheelchair,

we walked

past the freak show

to the big top:

Mickey with one leg missing,

Charles with an arm

dead as an old fish,

me with one eye gone.

Past people who couldn't see

the wounds

that haunt our nights.

Eddie "Freak Man" Carlyle

Sideshow Fan

I came to see the freaks.

Can't have a midway without 'em.

Without the barker's call:

Hurry, hurry, hurry!

Step right up!

Friends and fans of freak shows,

see mysteries to beguile the innocent,

to confound the doubtful!

But this one's a bust.

Freaks

aren't what they used to be.

'Bout all they've got here are

a giant and his wife,

a fat girl,

Rasmus Neilson,

the tattooed strongman,

and a bunch of midgets.

Give me some *real* freaks.

Like Violet and Emily, Siamese twins

that played violin and piano,

like the half-girl Violetta,

nothing there from the waist down.

Give me a three-breasted woman

or an alligator man.

Give me the old days

when freaks were freaks:

Skeets Hubbard,

who drove a six-inch spike

into his forehead,

or Sealo, the seal boy.

How can you have a freak show

without a seal boy?

Circus's goin' to hell,

you ask me.

Give me the old days.

We had real freaks then.

David Hancock

Seatman

I didn't like it.

But I couldn't say nothing

'cause I'm just a seatman

working the grandstands

filling water buckets

watching for fire.

I understood my place.

But I knew

something bad would happen

when we pulled into the siding

so late we had to blow the evening show.

Everybody knows blowing a show's

bad luck.

Just like whistling in the dressing room

or peanuts on the floor

or them old camelback trunks.

Only worse.

Everybody knows that.

Just ask around.

Go 'head.

Just ask.

Anne Bibby

Thirteen Years Old

I kept telling myself

it wasn't her fault

that she had to work

and couldn't take me to the show.

"Work comes first,"

were her exact words,

"especially with your father away"

("fighting the war," she never said).

I kept telling myself

it wasn't her fault

as I watched

my best friends—

Jane, with hair the color of pennies,

Sally, a head taller and blond—

trying hard not to be excited,

turn and wave.

My words,

"Don't go,"

no more than a whisper,

were lost in the jolly music

that drew them

from me

until they were swallowed

by the tent's black mouth.

And I was left

blinking

in the July sun.

—PART 2—

Mabel Conrad

Animal Trainer

I thought a tiger's swipe

was fast

until I saw the fire spread.

It was like a dam burst —

water rushing

with no purpose

except to move.

I'd just finished my act —

working six jags,

all jumping from perch to perch

up their pyramid

until the highest was twelve feet above me,

hissing, snarling,

impatient to taste me —

when the screams started

and the tent became a sheet of flame.

I whipped my cats

into the runway chute

that ran through an exit

to a waiting truck.

Two got through

before the rest froze

distracted by the curtain of heat

the crush of people

desperate to get over the chute

snarling and screaming

fear and pain driving them.

My cats had a better chance than the people

who couldn't climb

fast enough

high enough

to save themselves

from the rush of other people

whose fear made them climb over bodies

whose final fearful breath had been wrung out

by the weight of desperation.

Martin K. Davies

Bandleader

I played silver cornet

in Buffalo Bill Cody's

101 Ranch Show,

played until charming Billy passed in '17.

I've been working the band

under the big top since '19.

Never missed a show.

Not a one.

Not even when I got ptomaine poisoning

the year we swung through Kansas,

which surprised me,

that ptomaine,

since I didn't usually eat in places

roughnecks and roustabouts favor.

I loved to put on the white uniform

with its gold epaulets and piping,

climb up on stage,

and have twenty-nine musicians

looking right at me.

They had to

because we had to switch our music

on a couple hundred cues during a show,

not just from act to act

but depending on

what happens in the act.

If somebody flubs a part

we come to the rescue

with loud music.

Rumba, ragtime, fox trot for the cat acts.

A lot of folks think

the horses dance to our tune.

Not so.

We play our tunes

to the way they dance.

There's only one song

I hate to play:

"The Stars and Stripes Forever."

It's got nothing to do with politics.

It's more to do with trouble,

it being the song every circus band plays

when something horrible happens.

As soon as I saw the flames

and heard those shouts

that's the song we started,

loud as we could

even though we didn't know

how terrible

things would get.

We played

until our uniforms blackened with soot

and our gold buttons

were too hot to touch.

Bill Conti

Parent

I yanked Danny

through the crowd.

Packed together,

we surged

except for those who fainted.

They got stepped on.

Couldn't help it

though I tried.

Danny was crying

when we reached the chute.

I tossed him

over to the other side

yelled for him to run

to meet me at the car.

He wailed but went.

I couldn't.

Not then

not with all the other kids

looking like small frantic dolls.

So I started tossing them

over the chute.

I didn't have to tell them to run.

I climbed atop the chute

grabbing any small hand

raised my way.

I just hauled them—

couldn't count how many—

up and over.

Up and over.

Until my foot slipped.

I lost my balance,

went down.

The crowd dragged me under
even though I raised my hand
for help.

Donald Hutchinson

Thirteen Years Old

I didn't know what was happening.

I was under the bleachers

like Uncle Eddie had told me,

searching for treasure.

I'd scooped

three quarters,

a half-eaten Baby Ruth bar,

and a linen handkerchief

with the initials *NVE*

in a small heart of red flowers.

Then I saw the usher

rushing at me

like I was a fox in his hen house.

The screams stopped him

as sure as if someone

had ahold of the back of his trousers.

That's when I smelled the fire.

Falling folding chairs clattered—

people thundered down the bleachers,

diving beneath near me

their faces drained by fear

as they fought to get through

the sidewalls of the tent.

Only they couldn't

until I remembered

the fishing knife in my pocket.

I clicked it open

leaped to the sidewall

and stabbed at it

then dragged the silver blade to the ground.

People shoved me aside

lurched through the widening slit

without a look at me.

I was lucky to find my knife

before I tumbled out

into the bright sun.

I still smelled that fire smell

as I stumbled

among the dazed

clowns carrying buckets of water

past circus wagons

once red yellow orange

bright as morning

now blistering

dark as the smoke.

John Cookson

Usher

I was a greenie

new to the show

since Pittsburgh last year.

I was supposed to watch for

kids sneaking in,

help old folks with canes.

Nobody told me to watch for fire.

But I couldn't miss it.

Not after people started pointing

to the screaming bleachers.

Then running.

And worse.

Oh, it took my breath away

the way they bunched up

at the animal chutes

and couldn't get over them

fast enough.

Anybody that couldn't keep up

was pushed aside

like an old chair

or trampled.

One man in a sailor uniform

punched another man

so he could get over the chute.

A boy dropped his glasses,

bent to get them.

I never saw him surface again.

Hats and purses fell like rotten fruit.

One man with thick arms and a Yankees cap

didn't budge from the top of the chute

until he snatched up his son

from the mob by his suspenders.

And the cats in the chutes

were growling and yelping

but you could hardly hear them

with the screaming

and the roar of the fire

like the fires of hell.

Joan Sutton

Twelve Years Old

How could the Wallendas do it,

balancing on a skinny wire like that?

How much practice did it take?

That's what I was thinking

when I heard somebody shout, "Fire!"

Only it wasn't really loud

just loud enough

to get people charging

out of the bleachers.

I saw the empty rows behind us.

"This way!" I shouted to Mom.

"You go!" she shouted back,

not able to keep the worry from her eyes,

before she was swept away by the rush,

holding Carl's left hand in her right,

her black leather purse

hanging from the crook of her left arm.

So up I went

to the top row,

had just enough time to look back

but Mom and Carl

were lost in the crowd

like tree limbs swept away in a mad river.

That's when I decided to jump.

I reached out

grabbed hold of the edge of the tent

swung free of the bleachers

hung for a heartbeat

maybe two

then flew into the sunlight

hit the ground

already tumbling forward

into a somersault

that spun me free.

Mrs. Estelle Sutton

Mother of Carl and Joan

If you'd like to know the truth

I didn't want to come to the circus.

Never liked them much.

Too dirty, smelly.

Too many "undesirables" lurking.

The circus seems to attract them

like pigs to mud.

But the children were blue,

missing their father,

who's been fighting

somewhere in France.

We had no idea when he'd return.

I told them not to worry

there'd been no letter

in twenty-six days.

He was just too busy

fighting those nasty Krauts.

How I curse them all

every night until I'm almost too tired

to pray for Roy's return.

It's been hard on us all

especially the kids,

who wonder why

their daddy's fighting

thousands of miles from home

while other dads are working

up the highway in the aircraft engine plant

and come home every night

for family supper

and comedy on the radio.

So I told them we'd go to the circus.

Joan was old enough to know

what I was doing

but Carl couldn't stop talking

about the wild animals he'd see.

He was so happy.

Then the fire started.

I never doubted we'd get out

all of us

and have a tale to tell Roy.

Now

he'll have to hear about us

from strangers.

Ralph Nesbitt

Eighteen-Year-Old Animal Trainer

I was working the elephants

near the main tent

when the fire started—

a lick of flame

in the top of the tent.

My first thought was,

How're those people going to get out of there?

Then somebody yelled,

"Get the elephants out!"

Nobody wanted 'em to charge the crowd.

I started shouting,

"Tails! Tails!"

and the herd lined up

tail-to-trunk

just like they'd been taught.

I was too scared to be proud of them.

We marched them out,

prodding them with bull hooks

when they dawdled.

I kept one eye on the herd

one on the tent,

black smoke pouring out

like from a hundred locomotives

and wondered again

about those poor people:

How're they ever going to get out of there?

When the herd was safe,

I cried.

Dennis Mortimer

Firefighter

We laid nine hundred feet of hose

then another hundred and a half.

About a ton of hose.

But we all knew

we were too late.

There was no tent

just folding chairs

and bleachers blazing

like nobody's business.

Too hot to get close.

See, they dip

their chairs in paint

and hang them up to dry,

so as the years pass

they're adding another layer of paint

eager to burn.

But that's not half the problem

of the tent itself.

To keep the rain out

they coat the canvas

with paraffin mixed with gasoline,

laid on good and thick with stiff brooms.

Oh, that waterproofs it all right—

been doing it that way for years—

but what does it give you?

One huge candle

just waiting for a light.

Jake Polansky

Circus Chief of Police

They still call me "Barnum Red"

even though my hair's white as snow.

Thirty years a circus chief of police

will do that to a fella.

Thirty years of looking for trouble

punks

drifters

cons on the run,

kids with parents who beat them

or ignore them,

kids who hunger

for the excitement of circus life.

The thrill lasts

until a roustabout swipes their wallet

or they have to work as cage boys

pushing wheelbarrows full of hunks of meat

as big as your face

to the cat cages.

We'd been lucky with this show.

Nobody'd gotten knifed or shot.

Our worst time was '42,

the fire in Cleveland.

Before you could say Jack Robinson,

the tent went up like a barn on fire.

Nobody was killed

but we lost about fifty animals.

We thought we had the two bums

that lit the match

but one was a liar

the other too feeble to know the truth.

But even he would have known

the truth of this fire.

The truth of screams.

And as wild as the flames,

the truth of final fright.

—Part 3—

Simon Goldman

Barbour Street Resident

This is a good neighborhood.

Look around.

Oh, the houses might not be as fancy

as those on the other side of town,

but *people* make a neighborhood.

And we got the best.

Mrs. Larrabee,

she must be eighty,

can hardly hear,

but she didn't need to hear

to help people.

She could see

those crying kids,

so she started passing out sugar cookies

pouring milk for those that'd have it.

People started lining up

outside the Pruitt place

when they heard he had a phone

they could use.

Sam Pruitt turned his back

when people offered nickels

to make a call.

People in line were crying

worrying out loud.

Kids who couldn't find their parents

gathered at 122

where Sally Beale,

new to the neighborhood,

tried salve and kind whispers.

Crazy old Mrs. Nesterenko

cut up potatoes

and laid the slices on burns

muttering in her Russian English

how this worked in the big war.

John Mays

tore up sheets for bandages

while his wife

in her wheelchair

sewed a silver button

on a red dress for a scared girl.

And down at Jasper's Pharmacy

old man Jasper,

though no one could accuse him

of passing out too many smiles,

passed out ice-cream sandwiches

for kids whose parents stood in line

to use the pay phone.

Somebody even said they saw him

spreading ointment

on the arms of kids

while he hummed

"Somewhere over the rainbow."

So, you can take your fancy houses.

I'll take what's in the hearts

of the people who live on this street.

William Harvey
State Trooper

As the bodies arrived at the armory

I tied green casualty tags to their toes.

We separated the bodies by sex

as best as we could tell

setting each on a sagging army cot.

Mostly women, though,

and older girls

filled three rows.

We put the children in one corner,

men in the middle.

Then I wrote a list for each victim:

any clothes or jewelry,

scars, tattoos,

dental work.

Anything that would help.

A soldier covered each corpse

with an olive drab blanket

as those searching lined up outside

in the shade of the elms.

When they came

searching for their dead,

they were escorted

by a state trooper and a nurse

to the area most likely to hold

their loved ones.

Nurses carried smelling salts.

We had three first-aid stations.

A rolling cart with coffee.

There was little noise.

Shuffling feet, sobs mainly.

The lucky ones found their dead

in the first few rows of cots

before they got to the back rows

where bodies looked

like solemn museum statues

except faceless and black.

I had pity for the searchers

who couldn't recognize their dead

and needed to start

the march

again

at the first cot

shuffling and sobbing.

Dr. Rose Beekman

Fire Expert

Surprised?

Oh, I'm sure

they were surprised

that the fire spread

so fast,

a runaway train.

Roared like one, too.

How fast did it spread?

Let me put it this way:

some didn't have time

to scream for help

before flames shot up

the side of the tent

like a dragon roaring to life.

Did they have a chance?

Not really.

Not the ones closest to the fire.

It'd be like surviving a volcano.

Hair sizzled.

Skin burned.

The tent became a chimney.

How long did it last?

Six minutes. Maybe ten.

Yes, I'm sure.

But for most it lasted

only long enough

to have the breath burned out of them.

Most of them were dead

long before black chunks of tent

fell on their bodies

like pieces of night.

Thomas Gallagher

Detective, Hartford Police Department

Her face caught my eye.

She was pretty

maybe six

about the age of my son.

Her green toe tag read #1565.

Untouched by the fire

except for a burn

on her neck and face.

Blond hair,

shoulder length and curly.

I pictured her blue eyes.

Wearing black patent leather shoes

part of a white flowered dress,

she was placed in the first row

because everybody thought

she would be the first

one claimed.

She wasn't.

Over 175 went before her.

In fact, no one came for Little Miss 1565.

Except William LeBlanc.

He took her

to Morrisette Funeral Home

where they cleaned her face

combed her hair,

took two more pictures,

just in case.

Two days later, they laid her in a small white coffin,

the last one available.

No one came for her.

LeBlanc drove her to Northwood Cemetery

through the black iron arch

past rows of empty graves,

marked with gray stones

telling tales of men

who died far from home—

Killed in Action

Missing at Sea—

their bodies as gone

as their hopes in life.

With all the burials—

fifty-four at Northwood—

the gravediggers

weary and sweating

needed to do

some final digging

while a solemn crowd waited.

A reverend read the Twenty-third Psalm.

A rabbi read the Kaddish.

A priest read in Latin,

sprinkled holy water.

In the sun

I waited with her

while the others left.

Even as she was lowered

into the ground

and dirt thumped on her coffin

no one came for her.

In the sun

I waited with her.

Robert James Summers

Accused of Setting the Fire

They wanted to know

who started the fire

so I told them.

I did.

I had to

because of the burning man I saw.

My mother said it was a dream

but I think she's wrong.

I *saw* the burning man.

He told me

I had to start the fire

or I would burn.

Oh, I believed him.

Yes, I did.

That's why I lit up

two barns and a garage

before I skipped town with the circus

running away from the burning man.

He scared me.

Yes, he did.

Sometimes he scared me

so much

I had to hurt children

and hide.

I'd close my eyes

until everything was night

but he'd pop up

like a jack-in-the-box.

I had to light a match.

Then a flaming horse

would charge out of the fire

with the burning man

chasing me.

Only I couldn't hear them

because their feet never

touched the ground.

I swear to that!

I was so afraid

they'd burn me up.

That's why

I set those fires.

I had to.

I didn't want to burn up.

Jane Washington

Police Property Room Clerk

I didn't go to the circus

but I could tell who did

from the things

that came here.

Mostly women and kids,

judging from the pile of pocketbooks

and the styles of the small shoes.

Everything gets tagged

and cataloged

then put under lock and key.

Eyeglasses

bank books

a rosary

ration stamps

don't ask me how much money —

some coins purple from the heat

half a ten spot, its edges black—

marbles

false teeth

buttons

a pair of fountain pens.

It all comes here

and we take care of it

as we listen to the radio,

hear the names of the dead

read

slowly

like prayers at church.

Donald Garrity Sr.

Parent

We didn't know

what to think.

Only that Donald didn't return

with the others.

A cousin cried that he was dead.

A neighbor said he ran from the fire

headed for the woods.

From what we'd heard on the radio,

we believed the worst

and headed for the armory.

Alice couldn't bear to look

so I went

alone,

sickened

by the smell of charcoal,

by the blackened burden on each cot,

relieved that Donald wasn't there.

Relief soured

when he wasn't at two hospitals either.

At Municipal

Alice stayed in the car

dabbing her eyes with a balled tissue

while I searched for my son.

The first nurse I saw in the lobby

I stopped

and asked about Donald.

"Please help me."

Bone weary,

she tried to smile,

asked me to wait.

I paced a line in the tile floor

until she returned.

"This way," she said,

leading me to the elevator.

She jabbed 5

and we lifted with a lurch.

I willed myself

not to ask

if Donald was dead.

On 5 we walked to 509

where she left me

to wipe my hands

on the seat of my pants.

Before I could move

the door swung in

and a nurse wheeled out

a body covered

with a sky blue hospital sheet.

I wouldn't believe

that I'd come this close

only to miss Donald.

I walked in.

The floor tilted

like the deck of a ship in a squall,

then righted itself

when I saw him

lying in bed

but smiling to see me.

We talked—

we must have—

but don't ask me about what.

He was bandaged—

hands, arms, back—

but he was going to make it,

skin grafts more than likely,

but he was going to make it.

"Where's Mom?" he asked.

"Oh, jeez, she's in the car."

We laughed.

"I'd better see to her.

She could use some good news."

Sally Weissman

Nurse

Nothing I'd seen in the ER

for seventeen years prepared me.

I'd seen burn victims

but these people...

I even thought—

God help me for saying it—

that the dead were the lucky ones.

It wasn't just the wounds—

the skin hanging off in sheets

peeled patches red as a good steak,

wounds weeping—

but the sounds—

children crying

parents wailing

shouting, "Help my baby!"—

the smell

of roasted flesh.

But there is always one case—

ask any of the girls in the ER—

that breaks your heart

wide open.

One woman

her face smudged

but hard with fear

grabbed my wrist

as I rushed by.

"Please," she said,

"check on my son.

He's my only one."

I had other patients to see

but she wouldn't let go of my wrist

until I promised

to look for her boy.

I found him among the other children

just as his last breath puffed out.

I held my breath

let it out

brought it back

before I reported the death to a doctor

who'd inform the mother.

Hospital policy.

Which I was glad for,

not having the heart

to not tell her

I was there

for his final sigh.

Jimmy Duncan

United States Marine Corps

I was stationed at Bradley.

Waiting.

That's what most of us were doing.

Waiting for mail.

Waiting to go over.

Waiting to go home.

So when I was ordered to a truck

to help at the fire

we'd been hearing about on the radio

I was glad to stop waiting.

The big top was gone.

The ground was black

like the smoke I could smell.

Long tent poles were scattered.

Some neatly side by side

some creasing the cat cages

others bashing the bleachers.

Cops walked around.

Animals raised hell in the distance.

Guys in summer suits

stood with their hands on their hips

looking.

MPs walked through the black,

picking up clothes and purses,

filling trash cans and cardboard boxes.

I turned when a lieutenant gave me

my orders for the day:

"You're with the G.I. party"

which puzzled me

since this was no place for a party.

When I followed him

to the rest of the Marines,

a lance corporal filled me in:

"G.I. means Graves Identification."

We didn't say a word

as we walked the black

where the big top used to be

looking for bodies

or worse,

parts of bodies.

In the hot sun we searched.

And found.

Back at Bradley

I walked alone

in the black night

waiting to forget

the little bodies

that I'd carefully carried.

That I still carried

into the pink dawn.

Sam Tuttle

Camera Operator

I still remember that day,

how hot it was

even before the fire.

I brought my new 8mm movie camera

to see how it'd work

to see if I could catch something special.

I filmed the midway

the menagerie

scenes filled with smiling faces

kids shrieking for joy

jabbering with excitement

hawkers selling souvenirs

barkers calling out

the names of their freaks.

I never had time

to see the show.

I was aiming my camera

at the tent,

smiling

as I zoomed in and out

to capture the size of the big top.

That's when I saw the corner

of the tent flash into flames.

I was so surprised

I took my eye away from the eyepiece

needing to make sure

the lens wasn't playing a trick on me.

Then the screaming started

people streaming from the tent

faces pained with fear

as black smoke blossomed

over the tent

like a tree of death.

I'm not sure

how long I filmed.

Enough to capture too much terror.

I know that.

We tried to save

as many people

as we could.

The fire investigators

searched my film

over and over

trying to spot someone to blame.

Eventually

they returned it.

I watched it once.

Enough to sicken me again.

But when I reversed the film,

killing smoke vanished

flames flickered to nothing

people backed out of the big top

and boys screeched with joy

jabbered in excitement

girls skipped and twirled

in their summer dresses

mothers smiled to see their children

joyous

all in silence,

none knowing

they would be this happy

for the last time

in their lives.

Note

On Thursday, July 6, 1944, as the afternoon perform-
ance of the Ringling Bros. and Barnum & Bailey Circus in Hartford, Connecticut, had just begun, fire
broke out in the southwest corner of the big top.
The fire was fast and angry, killing 167 people—
mostly women and children—in a matter of minutes
and injuring about 500 others.

Although the police determined that the fire was
caused "by the carelessness of an unidentified smoker
and patron who threw a lighted cigarette to the
ground," the real cause of the fire is still in doubt.
Stewart O'Nan believes the fire started near a port-
able toilet, but higher on the canvas wall. A man did
confess to setting the fire. However, his mental state
calls his version into question.

ACKNOWLEDGMENTS

I got the idea for this book about twenty years ago, although I didn't know it at the time. I read *The Chances We Take* by Richard Goldhurst (Baron, 1970), a novel based on the Hartford circus fire. What stuck in some corner of my mind was the fate of Little Miss 1565. Fast-forward to 2001, when that memory led me to read a brand-new book called *The Circus Fire* by Stewart O'Nan (Anchor, 2001), a fascinating nonfiction account of the tragedy. He mentions *Masters of Illusion: A Novel of the Connecticut Circus Fire* by Mary-Ann Tirone Smith (Warner, 1994), which I also read. By the time I had read (and reread) these books, I was ready to write my poems.